Wherever You'll Be

ARIELLA PRINCE GUTTMAN   GENEVIÈVE GODBOUT

FLAMINGO BOOKS

FLAMINGO BOOKS
An imprint of Penguin Random House LLC, New York

First published in the United States of America by Flamingo Books,
an imprint of Penguin Random House LLC, 2021

Text copyright © 2021 by Ariella Prince Guttman
Illustrations copyright © 2021 by Geneviève Godbout

Visit us online at penguinrandomhouse.com.

Library of Congress Cataloging-in-Publication Data is available.

Manufactured in China

ISBN 9780593206539

1 3 5 7 9 10 8 6 4 2

Design by Opal Roengchai
Text set in P22 Stickley Pro
The illustrations were created with pastels and colored pencils

To my little loves, Amalia and Adam
And to my sweetheart, Michael
My dreams came true with you
—A.P.G.

To my mom
—G.G.

Good morning, my sweet.
There's a new day ahead.

Let's get ready together.
Now jump out of bed!

The day will go fast
And be full of great things.
I'll miss you, of course,
But what fun today brings!

Wherever you'll be . . .

I'll be thinking of you.
I'll give you a kiss.
You give me one too.

At school with your friends
You'll sing a new song.
Your teacher will have
You dancing along.

You might learn a new word.
I'll learn something too.
I'm excited to hear
The new things you can do!

If today you feel sad,
Please try not to cry.
Just think of us singing
Our sweet lullaby.

Wherever you'll be . . .

I'll be thinking of you.

I'll blow you a kiss.

You blow me one too.

We'll both have our lunch,
And I packed you a snack.

The day is half over,
And soon I'll be back.

You'll swing at the park,
Jump, skip, and run.
And tonight tell me everything
About your day in the sun.

It's the end of the day.
We're together again.
You'll show what you've learned,
Like counting to ten!

You'll sit on my lap,
And we'll read a good book.
After such a long day,
How sleepy you look.

The moon shines so bright,
And now time for bed.
Tomorrow we'll do it
All over again.

Remember, my love . . .

Wherever you'll be,

I'm there with you too.

Just blow me a kiss.

I'll send one to you!